Acting Edition

Barrio Hollywood

by Elaine Romero

SAMUEL FRENCH

ISBN 978-0-573-66259-1

www.concordtheatricals.com
www.concordtheatricals.co.uk

FOR PRODUCTION INQUIRIES

UNITED STATES AND CANADA
info@concordtheatricals.com
1-866-979-0447

UNITED KINGDOM AND EUROPE
licensing@concordtheatricals.co.uk
020-7054-7298

Each title is subject to availability from Concord Theatricals Corp., depending upon country of performance. Please be aware that *BARRIO HOLLYWOOD* may not be licensed by Concord Theatricals Corp. in your territory. Professional and amateur producers should contact the nearest Concord Theatricals Corp. office or licensing partner to verify availability.

This work is published by Samuel French, an imprint of Concord Theatricals Corp.

MUSIC AND THIRD-PARTY MATERIALS USE NOTE

IMPORTANT BILLING AND CREDIT REQUIREMENTS

BARRIO HOLLYWOOD had its professional World Premiere at New Theatre, Coral Gables, Florida, Rafael de Acha, Artistic Director; Eileen Suarez, Managing Director, on October 14th, 2004. The creative team included movement director Ricky J. Martinez, set designer Michael McKeever, lighting designer Pedro A. Remirez, sound designer Ozzie Quintana, production stage manager Joseph M. NeSmith. Eileen Suarez provided photography. The production was directed by Rafael de Acha with the following cast:

GRACIELA MORENO . . . . Beatríz Montañez
ALEX MORENO. . . . . Euriamis Losada
AMÁ . . . . Marta Velasco
MICHAEL . . . . John Baldwin

BARRIO HOLLYWOOD was first produced at Borderlands Theater, Tucson, Arizona, Barclay Goldsmith, Producing Director, on March 27th, 2003. The creative team included ballet folklórico coach Karl Rodriguez, boxing coach Vicente Medina, choreographer Eva Tessler, set designer John Longhofer, lighting designer John Dahlstrand, sound designer Jim Klingenfus, costume designer Carmen Gastelum, stage manager John Sweeney, and production stage manager Glenn Stockellburg. The production was directed by Kent Nicholson with the following cast:

GRACIELA MORENO . . . . .Marissa Garcia
ALEX MORENO. . . . . Mario Figueroa Lopez
AMÁ . . . . Rosanne Couston
MICHAEL . . . . Dana Jepsen
SHADOW BOXER . . . . Eduardo Vega

BARRIO HOLLYWOOD was subsequently produced by the Miracle Theatre Group, Portland, Oregon, Olga Sanchez, Artistic Director Miracle MainStage, José Eduardo González, Founder and Executive Director, Dañel Malán, co-founder and Artistic Director Teatro Milagro, September 26th, 2003. The creative team included dance coach Sylvia Malán-González, fight coach, John Armour, set designer Mark Loring, lighting designer Peter West, sound designer Gerardo Calderón, costume designer Virginia Belt, and stage manager Emily Carr. The production was directed by Olga Sanchez with the following cast:

GRACIELA MORENO . . . . .Ina Strauss
ALEX MORENO. . . . . .Ricardo Delgado
AMÁ . . . . .Nurys Herrera
MICHAEL . . . . Anders Liljeholm
SHADOW BOXER . . . . .Tom Eveland

BARRIO HOLLYWOOD was given a staged reading at San Diego Repertory Theatre under the direction of William A. Virchis with dramaturgy by Nakissa Etemad. The cast included Alida Gunn, Sol Castillo, Catalina Maynard, and James Newcomb.

The Spanish-language translation of ***BARRIO HOLLYWOOD*** was developed for PlayFest – The Harriet Lake New Play Festival at Orlando Shakespeare Theater, Orlando, Florida, and presented in both languages under the direction of Ricky Martinez, Patrick Flick, Director of New Play Development, Jim Helsinger, Artistic Director.

CHARACTERS

ALEX MORENO, a twenty-four year-old Latino boxer.

GRACIELA MORENO, Alex's older sister. A twenty-nine year-old ballet folklórico dancer.

AMÁ, their forty-eight year-old mother. Sometimes a little girl who never grew up. Has a difficult time facing things.

MICHAEL, a white man in his early thirties. Beautiful, but he doesn't know it. He is a medical resident.

TIME

1999

PLACE

Kino Bay, Sonora, Mexico and Barrio Hollywood, Tucson, Arizona.

SET

A flexible space upon which the play takes place. Scenes should move fluidly. Realistic set pieces should be kept to a minimum.

AUTHOR'S NOTES

Spanish words that are italicized should be pronounced in Spanish.

When Grace's lines are in ALL CAPS, she raises her voice. There is no build to these moments.

For Brad

ACT I

Scene 1

(Cinco de Mayo, May 5th. Lights come up on **ALEX MORENO**, *twenty-four, on one side of the stage in a Mexican boxing ring, indicated by a Mexican flag, and* **GRACIELA MORENO**, *twenty-nine, at Kennedy Park prepping for her dance. She wears a white Veracruz-style* ballet folklórico *dress with red trim.*

She lights the candle on her headdress. Alex warms up for his fight with his back to the audience. They start performing simultaneously. Graciela performs the ballet folklórico *dance, "*La Bruja.*" Graciela's dance and Alex's fighting are both slow and rhythmic. Their performances continue until Alex takes a blow to the left side of his head. He falls, but slowly gets up. He slugs some more until he gets knocked unconscious. Graciela looks over at him, seeing across the limitations of physical space.*

Soft blue light as Graciela holds her unconscious brother in her arms. The candle on her headdress is still lit. A distinct echo of Alex's little boy laugh against pitch black.)

Scene 2

(Later that day. White lights up to an institutional bright. The hospital. The light accentuates a brick/partial lime green wall – la migra *green.* AMÁ, *forty-eight and pretty, lays a silk handkerchief on the table. She whips a small votive candle in blue glass out of her purse. She lights it with a cigarette lighter. She fans herself with the smoke. She takes out a shaker of salt, shakes a handful of salt into her left hand and throws it over her right shoulder. She twirls three times. She claps her hands together. She puts them together in a prayerful position. She looks in both directions. Assured that the coast is clear, she pulls her rosary out of her bra and begins running the beads through her fingers. Whatever her movements are, she is clearly partaking in an idiosyncratic, eccentric ritual.)*

AMÁ. I'll say a rosary every day. I'll go to Mass every morning at five o'clock. I'll go to confession twice a week. Make it three. I'll fast every Friday, and not only during Lent. For just this one thing, God.

I don't ask for much. You know, I never do. I'm happy with what you give me. *Muy contenta* with your plan. *Tu camino loco. (She laughs.)* We know.

(A disturbing vision undercuts her laughter. Alex appears behind the scrim. The boxing bell rings, not once, not twice, but three times. Each time corresponds to a blow Alex takes to his head. It is as if Amá is stuck in that moment. She grabs her head.)

But that picture in my mind, *en mi mente. Mi hijo.* Flat like that. You can change that picture. I know you can. Alex will be fine, and kiss me on the cheek. *(Points to her cheek)* Right here. Right, God?

(Beat) Fifteen years with my husband. And fifteen without him. Years where he just drifted off. We waved goodbye to him from the front porch, me and *mis hijos*, but he did not turn around to say goodbye.

My husband, Ernesto, the only husband I'll ever have.

Oh, I am faithful to him. Like I promised. Even though he is not faithful to me.

Yeah. We gotta a deal, You and me.

(Amá gives God a knowing grin. **MICHAEL**, *an Anglo resident doctor in his early thirties, enters.)*

MICHAEL. Mrs. Moreno?

AMÁ. Yes.

MICHAEL. We've been checking on your son.

AMÁ. Yes.

MICHAEL. The doctors are looking him over right now.

(Michael references Alex's chart. He seems inexperienced in his role as physician.)

Currently, his condition is – indeterminable.

AMÁ. I don't know what you mean.

MICHAEL. *(Not sure how to simplify)* Um…

AMÁ. *(Gesturing)* Find a little word. A tiny word.

MICHAEL. I –

AMÁ. I want to know what's happening with my son!

GRACIELA. *(O.S.) (Responding to nurse)* Guadalupe Moreno. My mother.

(Graciela walks in stunned, white, scared. She wears her dance costume. Michael immediately takes notice.)

MICHAEL. *(To Graciela)* Hello, Miss.

AMÁ. My daughter.

GRACIELA. I – I – I –

MICHAEL. Just take a couple deep breaths.

GRACIELA. I – saw him.

AMÁ. *M'ija,* could you explain what the doctor means? I don't know what he means.

(Graciela grabs Michael's hand.)

GRACIELA. Hallway – bed. Door. They wouldn't let me in.

(Michael gently removes Graciela's hand. She sinks into a chair.)

AMÁ. *M'ija, m'ija, m'ija.*

GRACIELA. He – he – he –

AMÁ. Shhh.

GRACIELA. *(To Amá)* He – can't – talk.

> *(Graciela breaks out crying. Michael hands Graciela a Kleenex®. She blows her nose.)*

MICHAEL. There's no evidence of that.

AMÁ. Of course he can talk. He's been talking since he was eighteen months old. You should know, you taught him yourself. *(Imitating her)* Cookie, taco, refrigerator. *(To Michael)* His third word – refrigerator – she taught him that.

GRACIELA. I screamed, "Alex. Alex!" But he doesn't hear. Me. *(Pointing at herself)* Me.

MICHAEL. You need to believe he can hear you. It's very important you believe he can get better. Do you?

GRACIELA. I –

MICHAEL. Do you believe?

GRACIELA. I –

AMÁ. *(Innocently)* I believe.

GRACIELA. He can't say his name.

MICHAEL. It's really early to jump to those kinds of conclusions.

GRACIELA. He didn't answer…today. He didn't say, "Yes, Gracie. I can hear you. I'm still here." *(To Michael; piercing)* Is he still there?

MICHAEL. *(Taken aback; beat)* I – we don't know. *(Quickly)* When the swelling goes down, we'll be in a much better position to answer your questions.

GRACIELA. What swelling?

MICHAEL. In the brain. *(Quickly)* Now, don't worry. Brain swelling happens all the time with athletes.

GRACIELA. *(Overlapping with Michael)* God.

AMÁ. Shh. We're at the hospital.

GRACIELA. *(Pointing)* Your son's dying in there.

MICHAEL. He's not...dying. He's stabilized.

GRACIELA. *(Numb)* You saved him?

MICHAEL. *(Proudly)* I was on the emergency room staff when they flew him in. I guess you can say that.

GRACIELA. *(Rocking; still numb)* I heard it on the radio. They play the radio between sets at the park. They were playing a new song called *"Cheech's chones"* for Cinco de Mayo and everybody was laughing.

AMÁ. *(Singing)* "He don't wear no *chones*. Naa."

MICHAEL. And *chones* are?

AMÁ. *Underwears.*

GRACIELA. And then they made this announcement, about Alex Moreno, the state featherweight champion – how he was illegally boxing in Mexico and he got caught. 'Cause God doesn't let you cheat! *(Calmer)* It was a newsflash. *(Upset)* About my brother. And everything they said, doctor, did not give me the impression – THAT HE WAS OKAY!

MICHAEL. "Okay" would be too strong a word.

GRACIELA. "Okay" would be a lie.

MICHAEL. It would be.

GRACIELA. He got fucked.

MICHAEL. *(Under his breath)* It appears he did.

GRACIELA. *(Finally, the truth)* Thank you.

AMÁ. *(Distracting herself)* Doctor, you don't wear no *chones* neither, do you?

MICHAEL. I – *(Blushing)*

GRACIELA. When will we know?

MICHAEL. About my underwear?

GRACIELA. About Alex.

MICHAEL. I'm not sure. There may be complications.

AMÁ. You have to let me visit. I always can cheer him up. He says, "*Amá*, you make me laugh sooo hard I cry."

(Reality seems to be dawning on her.)

I want to see my little boy.

MICHAEL. *(To Amá)* You can see him as soon as it's safe, Ma'am.

GRACIELA. After the swelling goes down?

MICHAEL. Then.

AMÁ. I'm not leaving here until I see my son. Go, get him Graciela. Wheel him in.

GRACIELA. We can't, *Amá.*

AMÁ. Why not?

MICHAEL. It's best not to move him.

AMÁ. Bring him in here. Or, I'm going there.

(She gets up.)

MICHAEL. Mrs. Moreno. Your son is in critical condition.

AMÁ. *(To Graciela)* Why can't you do what I say? Wheel him in. *(Demanding like a child)* Why not? Why not?

GRACIELA. They don't know what's wrong with him.

AMÁ. What?

GRACIELA. It could be really bad. That's what they said on the radio. Wheelchair. Crippled. FUCKED UP.

AMÁ. You don't need to yell.

(Graciela grabs Michael by the collar.)

GRACIELA. I want to know what's wrong with my brother and I want to know now.

MICHAEL. We have no information.

GRACIELA. Well, maybe if you got your ass in there and started taking some tests, YOU WOULD.

AMÁ. *M'ija,* don't lose control. *(To Michael)* You don't know what happens when she loses control.

GRACIELA. I GO CRAZY!

(Graciela tightens her grip on Michael's collar.)

MICHAEL. *(Constricted breathing)* Stop.

(Graciela releases his collar.)

AMÁ. She gets a little upset. *(Loud whisper; to Michael)* It's that alcoholism. From her father.

GRACIELA. I'm not an alcoholic!

AMÁ. She's not an alcoholic.

GRACIELA. I'm not an alcoholic. Geez!

(Amá pulls Graciela into herself. Resting Graciela's head on her shoulder, she pats Graciela's head.)

AMÁ. We're gonna get over this. We've been through worse. Like when your father left.

GRACIELA. *(Matter-of-factly)* My father left.

AMÁ. So sad. The kids cried for two years, *¿qué no?* *(Matter-of-factly)* I'd run out of candles on my *altar.* That's why he left. Oh, he didn't know that was the reason, but that was why.

GRACIELA. So sad.

AMÁ. You got to keep those candles burning or *Nuestra Señora* won't look down.

MICHAEL. I'm sure after we've had a chance to examine him, we'll realize that everything is fine.

GRACIELA. *(Still a bit dazed)* I like that song, do you?

AMÁ. You should hear her sing, *Doctor.* She played *María* in the "Sound of Music" at Catholic school. Well, she was the understudy. And the other *María* got laryngitis. *(Singing with a laryngitis voice)* Y *cantó así.* *(Normal)* And they sent Graciela up. And she sang like an angel. Better than that Anglo girl.

GRACIELA. *Amá.*

AMÁ. You did. And everybody said, "Why didn't they give Graciela that part in the first place?" And the nuns, and I don't ever forget this, because we gave *las monjitas mucho dinero.* They said, they just couldn't see a little Mexican girl playing *María.* Her name was *María.* *(Louder)* She was a Mexican girl. *Son pendejas.* And they never taught you nothing, except *que el ingles* was *mejor que el Espanich.*

GRACIELA. *(Beat)* We'll sing that song for him. We'll bring him back to the world with something he loves.

AMÁ. Something he loves.

GRACIELA. Boxing. He loves her like a lover, he told me. He has no woman except her.

AMÁ. He has us. He doesn't need a woman.

GRACIELA. *(Quoting Alex)* "Boxing is in my blood. It's what keeps me alive, little sis."

(Graciela chokes up.)

MICHAEL. Everything's going to be fine. Candles or no candles.

(Graciela looks up at him.)

GRACIELA. I believe in you.

(Graciela and Michael's eyes catch. She entrusts herself to him.)

AMÁ. The candles are very important. The fire catches *La Virgencita's* attention. *Como una estrella.* The light guides her to see into your house – then your heart. That's why I always keep my candles burning. Don't I, *m'ija?*

GRACIELA. Oh she's a nut about it. The house glows like a church.

(Graciela smiles at the doctor, but Amá seems to be realizing something important.)

AMÁ. *M'ija,* you stole my candle today.

(Graciela seems taken aback.)

Para tu danza. You took *la protección!*

GRACIELA. That's crazy!

AMÁ. You did. *(Beat) Doctor,* I must see my son.

MICHAEL. You can see him through the glass.

GRACIELA. *Amá,* the Virgin wouldn't punish you like that.

AMÁ. It's an emergency. *¡Híjole!*

GRACIELA. *Amá,* don't overreact.

AMÁ. I want to see him in his room. Right now!

MICHAEL. Three minutes.

AMÁ. Five.

MICHAEL. This is not a negotiation. I'm breaking the rules.

(Amá quickly applies her lipstick, upset.)

AMÁ. *Estoy lista.*

MICHAEL. Excuse me.

AMÁ. *(Harried)* I'm ready.

MICHAEL. *Cinco minutos. Nomás.*

(Graciela looks surprised at the Spanish.)

Head nurse taught me that. It's tough to get you guys to leave your family members alone.

GRACIELA. Well, we don't just give up on each other.

(Amá stands up, grabs the doctor by the hand.)

AMÁ. *(To Graciela)* This is your fault.

GRACIELA. They're just candles!

(As Amá drags Michael out the door, he looks back.)

MICHAEL. You just wait right there. Make yourself at home.

GRACIELA. Okay.

(As they leave.)

MICHAEL. The swelling makes it look much worse than it is.

(Graciela drops her head in her hands, wringing her hair. She looks up. Her song is more along the lines of a show tune than a traditional Mexican song.)

GRACIELA. *(Singing)* Everything is fine. Everything is fine. *(Launching into the tune loudly)* EVERYTHING IS FINE *(Softer)* if only I'd believe it. *(Belting it out)* EVERYTHING, EVERYTHING, *(Spoken)* is fine.

(Graciela turns her head in both directions to look for listeners. Blackout.)

Scene 3

(Out of time. The stage is black. Amá lights a long match. It burns as a light comes up on her. She lays a blue star-studded cloth on the floor. Wrapped in the cloth are a round box of long wooden matches, a Virgin of Guadalupe religious candle, and a shaker of salt. She lights the candle, fanning herself with the smoke. She shakes a handful of the salt into her left hand and throws it over her right shoulder. She twirls three times. She claps her hands together. She puts them together in a prayerful position. When she looks up from the prayer, Alex and Graciela appear in separate light on both sides of her.

Each person partakes in his/her own sacred movement, boxing and dancing, respectively. There is something very dance-like about Alex's boxing and something very boxing-like about Graciela's dancing.

A game ensues: the three begin to move into each other's spaces, taking on each other's movement whether it be praying, boxing, or dancing. The frenzy ends when all fall to the ground as in a children's game. Alex's little boy laugh echoes in voice-over, ending abruptly.)

GRACIELA. You vanished. Like breath. I want to feel you again inside my lungs, like the steam of the peppermint tea *Amá* used to give us when we were sick. Because I am sick. So tired. So much older than me. I look in the mirror and watch myself turn thirty. That's when you finally, after all those years, become a real woman.

Scene 4

(Two months after Cinco de Mayo. Lights up on the Moreno home. Amá and Michael sit at the kitchen table. Alex lies flat on a hospital bed with wheels. An intravenous feeding tube is hooked up to his arm.)

MICHAEL. They have full-time nurses who really know what they're doing.

AMÁ. But will they give him love?

MICHAEL. They read to the patients and everything.

AMÁ. What do they read?

MICHAEL. *(Stumped)* I'm not sure.

AMÁ. I don't want them reading him some *gabacho* story that he doesn't understand.

MICHAEL. I'm sure they'll read him what he likes.

AMÁ. If he can't talk, how will they know what he likes? *(Disgusted)* Nursing homes.

(Michael has no response. Graciela walks in, immediately checks on Alex, adjusting a pillow to make him more comfortable.)

Here's the girl.

MICHAEL. Hi.

GRACIELA. *(Shyly)* Hi.

(This is obviously more than a house call. There seems to be some attraction here.)

Are you sure it's okay – you coming over here to visit?

MICHAEL. Alex isn't my patient anymore. I waited two whole months to even ask you out.

GRACIELA. I'm glad you did.

MICHAEL. You're glad I waited?

GRACIELA. No, called. *(Beat)* I loved that place you took me on Tuesday night.

MICHAEL. Club Congress?

GRACIELA. The girl in the cage. Really wild! I'd never have

the guts to dance half-naked and crazy like that. And
she was a homegirl.

MICHAEL. *(Embarrassed)* I didn't know they'd have people
doing that there. *(Quickly)* I loved *your* dance performance. Thanks for inviting me.

GRACIELA. Well, when you called to follow up on Alex, I
was really touched.

MICHAEL. I liked the way you had your hair up.

GRACIELA. Oh, that wasn't my hair.

MICHAEL. It wasn't? *(Disappointed)* Oh, I thought – *(it was)*

GRACIELA. I used to have hair like that. *(Wanting to please)* I
could grow it out again.

MICHAEL. It was really pretty on you, even if it was fake.

GRACIELA. Thanks.

*(Michael touches Graciela's hand, intertwines his pinkie
with hers. They just stare at each other. They clearly
want to kiss. Amá has to split up this mutual admira-
tion party. She clears her throat.)*

AMÁ. She changes the IV. She knows how to do it. Those
mechanical things confuse me. I've broken everything
Alex bought me.

GRACIELA. *(Explaining)* She broke the garbage disposal in
three days. On avocado pits.

AMÁ. *(A loud whisper)* I was making *guacamole.*

MICHAEL. *(Suddenly serious; to Graciela)* So, he's been the
same since he left the hospital?

GRACIELA. If you want to take a look – *(at him.)*

AMÁ. She's the one to ask. She watches him all day long.
She won't even look up at the television.

GRACIELA. *(Embarrassed)* Amá.

MICHAEL. It's beautiful. You care.

GRACIELA. Well, I know my brother. Like when he boxed,
he could beat the biggest guy in the world as long as
there were people cheering for him.

AMÁ. *(To Alex)* Go, Alex!

GRACIELA. *(Back to his question)* His eyes.

MICHAEL. What about the eyes?

GRACIELA. They open and shut. Once in the morning. When I lift the blinds and the sun gets in his face. And again after dinner.

MICHAEL. That's great.

GRACIELA. Amá and I have been trying to figure out what it all means.

AMÁ. I told her – it's a sign from God. When Alex wakes up, he'll walk over and give me a kiss right here. Won't you, *m'ijo?*

(Amá waves at Alex.)

¡Hola!

GRACIELA. And his toes. I saw him wiggle his toes a few times. That counts, doesn't it?

MICHAEL. Wonderful.

GRACIELA. I knew these were good signs.

AMÁ. I started lighting *La Virgen's* candles again to make up for that other time. On *Cinco de Mayo.*

GRACIELA. He gets better every day.

AMÁ. Give *La Virgen* time. *Con tiempo, ella siempre perdona.* With time, she always forgives.

MICHAEL. I'll have to talk to the neurologist about these signs, but I find any movement at all very, very encouraging.

GRACIELA. Encouraging. *(To Amá)* Did you hear that?

(Amá points at the casserole dish in the middle of the table.)

AMÁ. Have some *enchiladas.* Graciela made them. It's her specialty. Actually, it's the only thing she knows how to make.

GRACIELA. *(With a smile)* That's not true.

AMÁ. She uses a little *mole.* You won't taste them like that out of the freezer section.

MICHAEL. *(To Amá)* You first.

AMÁ. No. I'm just having a little salad.

(Amá reaches for a small bowl of salad, crosses herself, and begins eating.)

MICHAEL. You're not eating Graciela's enchiladas?

GRACIELA. Will you tell her that *woman* cannot live on lettuce alone?

AMÁ. I'm the only woman out of all of my sisters that doesn't have the *diabetes*. And you know why?

MICHAEL. You didn't inherit it.

AMÁ. No, you know really why?

MICHAEL. That's really why.

AMÁ. Because I watch my diet very carefully. What goes in and what goes out.

(Michael laughs.)

GRACIELA. *(Looking at Alex)* When Alex is thirsty, I give him ice cubes. That's the highlight of his day. Sheer oral pleasure.

(Graciela catches herself – she's embarrassed.)

AMÁ. She takes good care of him. I tell her she should go to school to become a nurse.

MICHAEL. Are you going to become a nurse?

GRACIELA. The dance school is my dream. Passing down the dance the way it was done by our ancestors. In little villages all over *México*. And never forgetting that it's all supposed to be fun. I'd forgotten that. But after Alex got hurt, I could hear him talking to me in my head. Like he was dead.

MICHAEL. You mean alive.

GRACIELA. I mean, dead.

AMÁ. The dead talk to us, you know.

GRACIELA. And he told me, "Gracie, you need to have more fun." *(Pained)* Because he loves me. And he wants me to be happy. He used to fill up this place with his laughing.

AMÁ. I think she should become a nurse. It's a good job.

MICHAEL. It's a solid job. You can work wherever you want.

GRACIELA. Like where?

MICHAEL. I don't know – New York, Miami, Michigan –

GRACIELA. Why the hell would I want to go to Michigan?

MICHAEL. I'm from Michigan.

GRACIELA. Oh, I see how this works. You know I just threw out that I'd consider nursing to make her happy and now she won't forget about it.

AMÁ. *(Hurt)* M'ija.

GRACIELA. Nurses, doctors, lawyers. *Amá*, we're from the most beat-up street in Barrio Hollywood. We don't have the money to become those kinds of things.

AMÁ. Alex has a little money saved. I'm sure he'd want you to follow your dream.

GRACIELA. *(Firmly)* My dream is to own a dance studio. *(Softens)* I like being a dance teacher. It makes me happy.

(Graciela walks over to Alex's bed by the window and moves him.)

MICHAEL. What are you doing with him?

GRACIELA. Giving him a different view.

AMÁ. He likes to watch the neighbors.

MICHAEL. Those *vatos* on their porch across the street smoking pot?

GRACIELA. It's part of his massage.

AMÁ. We give him a massage every night.

(Graciela walks over to Alex, focuses on him, starts massaging his arms. Amá massages Alex's feet.)

GRACIELA. It makes him feel more alive.

AMÁ. Because he is alive.

GRACIELA. *(Sarcastically)* That's why he hasn't said a goddamn word in two months.

AMÁ. She gets a little upset.

GRACIELA. *(Getting upset)* I do not get upset.

MICHAEL. Even for a few days, one of those homes might be nice.

AMÁ. Maybe he's right.

GRACIELA. We're not putting him in a home.

AMÁ. Listen to the *doctor.*

GRACIELA. He's a medical student.

MICHAEL. Resident.

AMÁ. It might be best.

GRACIELA. Alex is fine. He's got it made. He gets his massage every night at 6:30. Eats through that thing in his arm. He's just taking a time out. A breath.

(Graciela takes a deep breath in and out. Amá and Michael are transfixed by the breath as if Alex's fate is hanging on it. Graciela lines up a row of religious candles on both sides of Alex, lighting them one by one. There are two levels of window sills, so some of them are on both sides of Alex's head. Michael looks like he wants to ask a question. Amá stops him. It is a spiritual moment that should not be interrupted. Graciela puts her hands together, nods in prayer and returns to the dinner table.)

(To Michael) I'm sorry. I just want him to get well.

MICHAEL. *(Understanding)* I know.

GRACIELA. Maybe you could take a look at him –

AMÁ. After dinner.

GRACIELA. *(Continuing)* I know you're qualified. You saved him and everything.

MICHAEL. *(Not sure if he's been saved)* We did.

GRACIELA. It was the right thing to do.

AMÁ. Do you like the *enchiladas?*

MICHAEL. Yes. Delicious.

AMÁ. Why don't we feed some to Alex? He loves Graciela's *enchiladas.*

(Graciela and Michael look at each other uncomfortably. Alex is not conscious enough to eat. Amá starts to put a fork full of food up to Alex's lips.)

Eat up, *m'ijo.*

(A magical moment as a red light comes up on Alex. Alex opens his mouth, licks the enchilada, smacks his lips, shuts his mouth.)

GRACIELA. He moved!

(Graciela and Michael rush over. Graciela takes over the fork, starts trying to feed Alex the enchilada. Amá hangs onto Alex's feet, trying to wake him up. Alex lets out a huge burp. End of movement. They all try to wake Alex to no avail. He's out again. The red light fades.)

I believe. I believe.

AMÁ. Alex. Alex.

(They all stare at Alex, transfixed by what has just happened. Alex doesn't stir. Lights dim slightly on the tableau for a moment. Then, Michael begins to check Alex's vital signs. Michael slows down. There is no further movement from Alex. Amá seems the most distraught.)

GRACIELA. It's okay, *Amá.*

MICHAEL. *(Beat)* Do you think we all imagined it? *(Beat)* That really was an amazing amount of movement for –

GRACIELA. For what?

MICHAEL. *(Knows he's saying the wrong thing)* A comatose patient.

GRACIELA. *(Disappointed)* Oh.

AMÁ. Did you see him, *m'ija?* He wanted to eat dinner with us.

GRACIELA. He eats dinner with us every night, *¿verdad?*

AMÁ. The other night I went into his room and he was sleeping on his side. Like a baby. And I touched his forehead right there, and he smiled at me.

(Michael starts to interrupt. Graciela stops him.)

GRACIELA. It's Friday night, *Amá.* Poker night.

AMÁ. Why don't you two go out? Have another real date.

GRACIELA. No. You go out. Have your poker night.

AMÁ. Really?

GRACIELA. Yes, really. You deserve a break.

AMÁ. Are you sure?

GRACIELA. I'm certain. It's only one night, and we have a real doctor here to take care of Alex.

AMÁ. Well, you know I did very well last week.

GRACIELA. I'm sure you did. Now, go win.

AMÁ. *(Clearly cheered up)* Oh, thank you, *m'ija. (Amá looks at the dishes.)* Oh, the dishes.

GRACIELA. I'll get them.

(Amá smiles and leaves.)

She sees what she wants to see. Alex on his side. Smiles. Tears. It's all part of the movie in her head.

MICHAEL. Let her have her hope.

GRACIELA. It's senseless hope, isn't it?

MICHAEL. Hey, don't give up.

GRACIELA. Why not?

MICHAEL. Hope matters.

GRACIELA. She sometimes stops being an adult when it gets hard. She makes popcorn and goes into Alex's room and flips on the TV. Boxing. "It'll cheer him up, *m'ija.*"

MICHAEL. I've seen things. People recover who were supposed to be dead. Real miracles. When I was in that trauma unit that night, I didn't think we were going to save him.

GRACIELA. But you did.

(Michael touches Graciela's hand, comforting her.)

You make me strong.

MICHAEL. You make me strong, too.

GRACIELA. Why do you need to be strong?

MICHAEL. *(Embarrassed)* I don't know. It sounded good?

GRACIELA. You're funny.

MICHAEL. *(Beat)* I can get an appointment to talk to the neurologist next week.

GRACIELA. I'd appreciate that.

MICHAEL. It's gonna be okay.

GRACIELA. Yeah.

(Michael strokes her face. Graciela receives it.)

MICHAEL. You're amazing – the way you love him.

GRACIELA. It's just – normal.

MICHAEL. Maybe to you it is, but not to the rest of the world.

(Graciela smiles at him. Michael strokes her face, moves in and French kisses her. She enjoys it for a second and then pulls away. It is more of an awkward than a romantic moment.)

It's me. I'm hopeless with my tongue.

GRACIELA. It wasn't that.

MICHAEL. I was trying not to use my teeth.

GRACIELA. It's not that either. *(Long beat)* It's just I've never dated anyone like you before.

MICHAEL. What do you mean?

GRACIELA. Well, you're a doctor. Which means you have a job.

MICHAEL. Yeah.

GRACIELA. And you're tall.

MICHAEL. Yeah.

GRACIELA. *(Blurting it out)* And I've never dated an Anglo before.

MICHAEL. *(Disappointed)* Oh.

GRACIELA. It's okay. I've just never done it. It's not like I'm a racist. I'm open-minded.

MICHAEL. Okay, I believe you.

GRACIELA. I feel stupid for even bringing it up.

MICHAEL. No, it's worth bringing up.

GRACIELA. *(Beat)* You're very cute.

MICHAEL. Thanks.

(Graciela crosses to Alex, tucks in his sheet.)

GRACIELA. I'll just put him to bed.

MICHAEL. Graciela.

(Graciela turns.)

GRACIELA. Yeah.

MICHAEL. I like that we're different.

GRACIELA. You do?

MICHAEL. I don't know the rules here. I don't even know how to be polite.

GRACIELA. *(Happy)* Good.

(Graciela wheels Alex off. Michael picks up the plates and puts the leftover food onto one plate. He does the job with great care. Graciela moves back into the room unnoticed. She watches him.)

(Startling him) You do dishes.

MICHAEL. And I cook.

GRACIELA. Mexican food?

MICHAEL. My mother's meat loaf, but I can learn.

GRACIELA. Family secret?

MICHAEL. Betty Crocker.

GRACIELA. Tell me another –

MICHAEL. What?

GRACIELA. Secret.

MICHAEL. About my family?

GRACIELA. About you.

MICHAEL. *(Beat)* When I went to that dance, and you were wearing your dance costume with all the colorful skirts, I thought you were the most beautiful woman I'd ever seen.

GRACIELA. Naa.

MICHAEL. You were. And when you danced, with your face really serious like that, I thought, I know how to make that woman smile.

GRACIELA. *(Challenging him)* Yeah.

(Michael moves and kisses her tenderly and less aggressively. Graciela smiles. Lights fade.)

Scene 5

(A week later. Lights come up Graciela's front porch. Music blasts from a boom box. Michael and Graciela dance together. Michael stops. He talks to her over the music. Graciela's backpack sits on the porch.)

MICHAEL. I don't know how to do it now that you said I dance funny.

GRACIELA. I didn't mean anything by it. You've just got different...rhythm.

(Michael stops dancing.)

MICHAEL. Now, that's a way to get me to cut loose and dance. Gee, I think I'll just move here and explore my different rhythm, like a catatonic on heavy meds.

(Graciela laughs.)

GRACIELA. It's beautiful...in its own way. Like an irregular heartbeat. I'm behind you, Michael. Behind your aspirations to become a dancer.

MICHAEL. A true teacher at heart.

GRACIELA. Yes.

MICHAEL. So, don't laugh at me anymore. Teachers aren't supposed to laugh.

GRACIELA. *(She gestures)* Okay, no more laughing. Dance teacher's honor.

(They start gazing at each other.)

You're growing on me – like a fungus.

(She laughs.)

(Suddenly serious) You're growing on me. *(Beat)* I'm not very good at all this, having boyfriends and stuff.

MICHAEL. Oh, and I'm some Mr. Smooth Guy. I'll tell you a little secret. All those years in college and medical school – you can call a romantic dry spell. I don't think I even went to coffee with anyone in eight years.

GRACIELA. Yikes.

MICHAEL. So you, my darling, are the expert here.

GRACIELA. Wow, I thought –

MICHAEL. Embarrassing, but true.

GRACIELA. I feel guilty – about Alex.

MICHAEL. Hey, I don't like the way we met either. But the fact we met, that's what matters. And if we didn't meet...

GRACIELA. Yes.

MICHAEL. We wouldn't know each other.

GRACIELA. Yes.

MICHAEL. And that would be tragic because some people you're just supposed to meet. You're supposed to touch their lives and let them touch yours.

GRACIELA. And I'm a person like that?

MICHAEL. You are that.

GRACIELA. That's very sweet.

MICHAEL. Oh, don't call me sweet. That makes me feel like a real loser.

GRACIELA. You are not a loser. You saved my brother.

MICHAEL. *(Ambivalent)* I did.

GRACIELA. So, you're not a loser. We have Alex because of you.

MICHAEL. Yeah.

GRACIELA. What is it?

MICHAEL. You have Alex.

GRACIELA. Because of you.

MICHAEL. Do you really have Alex?

GRACIELA. He's right inside, silly. Hey, I almost forgot. You absolutely must try on the belt. No self-respecting male *folklórico* dancer would dare dance without the proper accoutrements.

(Graciela reaches into her backpack to pull out the belt. She can't find it. She starts rummaging through the backpack.)

Where is the darn thing?

(Michael grabs the backpack. She starts to grab back and a book falls out.)

MICHAEL. *(Reading the title)* Boxing and Medicine: Head Trauma and the Pugilistic Patient.

GRACIELA. *(Backing off)* I –

(She takes the book back.)

The librarian ordered it for me from some medical school. They're so good at helping. Give to your public library. I just thought if there was something I could learn, I ought to learn it. I just – just forget it.

MICHAEL. No.

GRACIELA. I mean this doing nothing thing. I just can't do the doing nothing thing. Is there someone out there who we can talk to?

MICHAEL. I don't know. That neurologist ended up canceling our appointment and then he left the country.

GRACIELA. Will you try somebody else?

MICHAEL. Can I have this?

GRACIELA. I didn't understand the medical jargon anyway. If you could make some calls – ask some questions –

MICHAEL. I'll call the editor of this book.

GRACIELA. Thanks. *(Beat)* Shall we try the belt?

(Graciela wraps a ballet folklórico belt around Michael's waist.)

Much better. Almost perfect.

MICHAEL. What would it take for me to be perfect?

GRACIELA. You are perfect. Shut up.

MICHAEL. I don't believe you.

GRACIELA. Believe me. You're perfect.

(Graciela rises to her toes to kiss him.)

MICHAEL. Wow.

GRACIELA. What?

MICHAEL. Did you feel the spark between our lips?

GRACIELA. *(Giggles)* You shock me.

MICHAEL. I shock you.

GRACIELA. We shock each other.

(Michael just holds her and holds her from behind.)

MICHAEL. I'm so glad I know you.

GRACIELA. But do you really know me? That is the question.

MICHAEL. Getting to know you.

GRACIELA. And if you really knew me, would you still want me?

MICHAEL. I can't think of anything more amazing than truly knowing you. All the crevices and uncharted places.

GRACIELA. Now, shut up and dance.

(Michael takes a couple of decent ballet folklórico steps. He stops, awaiting her approval.)

What do you want?

MICHAEL. Credit. They were pretty damn good.

GRACIELA. Pretty is not perfection. Keep working. You'll have to establish a regular rehearsal schedule in order to eradicate your deficiencies in dancing.

MICHAEL. Tomorrow. Same place? Same time?

GRACIELA. And wear something with belt loops.

(Michael laughs.)

(Suddenly more serious) I can count on you – to make those calls?

MICHAEL. Yes, of course.

GRACIELA. I just want to know that we've done everything we could.

MICHAEL. Of course.

GRACIELA. I miss Alex.

MICHAEL. If we could start at a different place, I'd give you that.

GRACIELA. Maybe it's the place that allowed us to start. Maybe some places open up spaces for extraordinary phenomenon like you and me.

MICHAEL. You are – extraordinary.

GRACIELA. You.

MICHAEL. What?

GRACIELA. Extraordinary. Beyond adjectives. Beyond comprehension.

MICHAEL. Me? Beyond comprehension?

GRACIELA. Like a big fat book with lots of stories intertwined. Complicated and thorough. Something that can be delved into like the sea.

MICHAEL. That's quite a compliment.

GRACIELA. Find us the right brain doctor and I'll have more.

MICHAEL. Agreed.

GRACIELA. I'll shower you with praise.

MICHAEL. You'll shower with me?

GRACIELA. In your dreams.

MICHAEL. I have an active imagination.

GRACIELA. Save it for later.

MICHAEL. When's later?

GRACIELA. For when Alex gets well and I can leave this house.

MICHAEL. Well, uh –

GRACIELA. I say a rosary for him every night. Two, actually.

MICHAEL. I've got to get going.

GRACIELA. Michael. Don't you believe?

MICHAEL. I don't know.

GRACIELA. Find out something. Do your homework.

MICHAEL. I'll take this with me.

GRACIELA. It's a library book. Bring it back. If I knew the right questions, I'd call myself. Maybe I should just –

MICHAEL. No, no. I'll do it, Graciela.

GRACIELA. Thanks.

(Michael gives her a quick kiss goodbye.)

I felt it that time. Your little spark.

(Are they establishing a little routine?)

MICHAEL. You shock me.

GRACIELA. You shock me.

MICHAEL. *(As he leaves)* We're shocking.

(Graciela laughs.)

Scene 6

(The morning of Cinco de Mayo. Lights quickly up on the Moreno home. Graciela ices Alex's head. He is sprawled out on the couch. He is groggy.)

ALEX. Not so hard.

GRACIELA. I'm not applying any pressure at all.

ALEX. I'm just a little dizzy.

GRACIELA. Is that why I found you lying face down on the bathroom floor?

ALEX. The tiles feel good on my face in the heat.

GRACIELA. It's not even summer yet. And I don't see you as the kind to roll around on tiles, like a dog, to cool off.

ALEX. *(A non sequitur)* Mexican tiles.

GRACIELA. *(Doesn't understand)* Yes, they're Mexican tiles. *(With humor)* You look like shit.

(Graciela waits for him to give his standard response.)

Aren't you gonna say, "So do you"? *(Beat)* You always say that.

ALEX. *(Truly not remembering)* I do?

GRACIELA. Yes, you always say, "So do you." It's one of our routines.

ALEX. Routines?

GRACIELA. What happened to you last night?

(Amá enters. She plays with her new vacuum cleaner. A gift, it still has a red bow wrapped around it. She vacuums every part of the house while singing "I Feel Pretty." She even tries to vacuum Alex and Graciela with the hose. Alex just smiles as she runs over him.)

(She grabs her necklace.)

Watch out! You could catch my cross in that thing. *(Screaming over the VACUUM.)* He isn't well. *Enfermo, Amá.*

(Graciela clicks the VACUUM OFF. Dead silence.)

AMÁ. *¿Qué qué qué?*

GRACIELA. You're always off in your own little world.

AMÁ. I like my little world.

GRACIELA. Look at him. He isn't himself.

ALEX. *(Singing)* "There's no business like show business like no business I know."

GRACIELA. *(To Alex)* Ever since we got home, you've been acting crazy like *Amá*.

(This clearly offends Amá. Alex motions for her to come over. She kisses Alex on the head.)

AMÁ. Is your head all better, *m'ijo?*

ALEX. You're the best, *Amá*.

(Alex starts kissing her and kissing her again on the cheek. It's a little much.)

AMÁ. *(To Graciela) Ella tiene celos.* We got good stuff now.

ALEX. Yeah, we got good stuff.

GRACIELA. You're lucky that *cabrón* didn't break your – *(nose)*

ALEX. I lose one fight and look at you.

GRACIELA. I don't want you to fight anymore, Alex.

ALEX. Christ! A guy's allowed to get knocked out for once in his life.

AMÁ. Yeah!

GRACIELA. You guys are driving me crazy.

ALEX. Go find yourself another family.

AMÁ. Yeah!

GRACIELA. I thought we agreed to not give her permission to do that.

AMÁ. Yeah!

GRACIELA. Stop it!

AMÁ. Yeah!

ALEX. Yeah yeah yeah yeah yeah yeah.

(Graciela covers her ears, visibly upset.)

GRACIELA. I've got to get out of here. I've got a performance.

ALEX. Go. Go perform.

(*Graciela steps out in her* ballet folklórico *costume. She wears a white dress with red trim and a fake braid. She balances a glass-encased candle, about three inches in diameter, on her head.*)

That's just gonna fall off your head on the way to the car.

GRACIELA. Will not.

ALEX. Will, too.

GRACIELA. (*To Amá*) Aren't you gonna come watch *me*, *Amá*? It's Cinco de Mayo – the most high-paying Mexican holiday of the year. Kennedy Park. *I* used to make you proud before that little *mocoso* came around.

(*Alex motions behind Graciela's head, indicating to Amá that she needs to get Graciela to leave.*)

AMÁ. I used to go watch you dance before the people got shot.

GRACIELA. Those were gang kids. The park has good security now.

(*Amá puffs her hair.*)

AMÁ. I don't want to get any bullet holes through my hair.

(*Amá smiles self-satisfied.*)

GRACIELA. (*As she leaves*) I'm outta here.

(*Graciela exits. Amá pulls Alex's boxing trunks out of her purse.*)

ALEX. I thought she was never gonna leave.

(*Alex puts his boxing trunks on.*)

AMÁ. Are you too fat?

(*Amá drags out a scale. Alex stands on it.*)

ALEX. This is bullshit. I haven't eaten in three days, and I haven't had a glass of water in four hours.

(*Amá hands him a razor. Alex looks at it confused.*)

AMÁ. Shave your *hairs*.

(Alex drags the scale to the hallway, starts taking his trunks off. He stands on the scale again.)

ALEX. That scale should be right. I bought it last week.

ALEX. *(O.S.)* Thank God.

(Graciela enters. The glass enclosing the candle on her headdress has indeed broken. She looks distressed, perhaps crying a bit.)

GRACIELA. *Amá*, look. Do you have another candle?

AMÁ. Only on my *altar*.

(Graciela looks with begging eyes. Amá resists.)

GRACIELA. Just this once.

AMÁ. No, *m'ija*. That's for *La Virgen*. You want me to take her candle and give it to you? What's she going to think? That's our protection – *para nuestra familia. ¡No!*

GRACIELA. I promise you I'll buy you some nice ones at Walgreens. I'll borrow it just for this afternoon, so I can do this dance from Veracruz. *La Bruja* – the one where I have to dance completely solo with a *pinche* candle on my head. *(For Alex's benefit)* I wouldn't have to do it if I had *a partner*.

AMÁ. Okay. Just this once.

(Amá crosses to her altar and takes down a small pink candle, encased in glass. She hands it to Graciela.)

Don't break this.

GRACIELA. I won't, *Amá*.

(Alex enters, busily wrapping his hand with tape, in his own world.)

You're fighting?

ALEX. Cinco de Mayo. Most highly paid Mexican holiday of the year.

GRACIELA. *(To Alex)* Tell her you can't do this.

ALEX. It's just this little weasel from Nogales. Nothing *El Lobo de Magdalena* can't handle. *No te preocupes.*

GRACIELA. Alex.

ALEX. You're doing your thing. I'm doing my thing, Gracie.

GRACIELA. Okay, *wa,* but I think you should have your head examined.

ALEX. It's my business.

GRACIELA. Whatever. Do what you want.

(*Graciela exits. Lights fade.*)

Scene 7

(The present. Michael arrives at the front porch.)

MICHAEL. Am I late for class?

GRACIELA. So?

MICHAEL. So what?

GRACIELA. Did you find anything out?

MICHAEL. Yeah.

GRACIELA. And.

MICHAEL. It's very complicated…

GRACIELA. Locked-in syndrome?

(Michael seems surprised she knows about this.)

MICHAEL. What?

GRACIELA. I was up half the night trying to figure out the possibility that Alex has this Locked-in syndrome thing – like it says in the book. It says that the patient can blink and that makes everybody, especially the family, think that the person's still in there but they're not.

MICHAEL. He's locked inside his body. I'm sorry, Gracie.

GRACIELA. That's Alex's name for me.

(Michael tries to hold her.)

People think, if you have a boyfriend, you really love him, and maybe you do, but your brother, that's someone who's been with you almost every day of your life – that's someone who stays with you no matter what – 'cause he's your brother.

(There is an awkward silence. Michael hands her a handkerchief. She wipes her eyes.)

MICHAEL. You might want to think about letting him go. When you feed him, you keep him alive.

GRACIELA. Yeah.

MICHAEL. Letting him die.

GRACIELA. Oh.

MICHAEL. Just think about it.

GRACIELA. He's got to be in there. Somewhere. *(Choking up at the end)* I'm not going to starve my brother and make him suffer! He's going to be okay.

MICHAEL. I wish that were true.

GRACIELA. He's my little brother; I'm supposed to take care of him.

MICHAEL. I am so sorry this happened.

GRACIELA. *(Retreating to the daze of her mourning)* I can still see him there.

(Alex boxes behind the scrim, agile and healthy.)

Fighting that first fight. Winning. He was beautiful to watch. The most beautiful boxer I've ever seen. It was because of the dance he was like that. I never found another dance partner like him after he quit. He moved like the wind. Have you ever watched the wind? The way it crawls into every little place unseen. And you know it's been somewhere because of how it changes everything around it.

MICHAEL. I'm sorry.

GRACIELA. *(Beat)* They really loved him in *México. El Lobo de Magdalena.*

MICHAEL. I've heard tell.

GRACIELA. Where?

MICHAEL. I've been known to watch a little Spanish television.

GRACIELA. Since when?

MICHAEL. Since I met you.

GRACIELA. You've been trying to learn Spanish?

MICHAEL. *Poquito.*

GRACIELA. Why?

MICHAEL. *(Beat)* I'm sorry to be the one to tell you the news.

GRACIELA. Well, I think maybe one of those little miracles you told me about might happen. You think?

MICHAEL. Sure.

GRACIELA. Say yes, Michael. It would really mean a lot to me if you said "yes" instead of "sure."

MICHAEL. *(More positive)* Yes.

GRACIELA. You're very kind when you lie.

MICHAEL. Now, don't go and ruin it.

GRACIELA. You're very kind. *(Beat)* Alex is never going to wake up again.

MICHAEL. *(Sadly)* He can't.

GRACIELA. Okay, *wa.*

(Lights fade.)

Scene 8

(The past, days before Cinco de Mayo. Lights come up to happy times on the beach in Kino Bay, Sonora, Mexico. SOUND of WAVES SPLASHING. Graciela dances ballet folklórico *on an upside down boat. She is trying to lift her brother's hand, so he will join her.)*

GRACIELA. C'mon.

(Alex resists like hell. Alex looks around. It appears that he might do it.)

It's not like anyone's going to see you.

(Alex holds his ground. He is not going to do it. Graciela slips, straddling the boat. It was not such a great surface to dance on anyway. They both break out laughing, especially Alex.)

ALEX. That was graceful, Gracie.

GRACIELA. You wanted to dance with me.

(Alex lifts his hands up in defense. Graciela smacks him. He reacts. Graciela quickly leans against Alex back to back. This is a game they've played before.)

Beat you to the ground. I'm faster.

ALEX. I doubt it.

(Graciela and Alex lower their bodies, bending their knees. Graciela slides past Alex easily.)

You cheated.

(Graciela lifts her hands in denial. They slide down back to back.)

Did I ever tell you I love you, little sis?

GRACIELA. Hey, I'm older.

ALEX. I'm taller.

(The mood shifts as they relax.)

GRACIELA. You did the right thing bringing *Amá* here. She loves the water.

ALEX. By the end of the month, we'll have lobster every day. Promise.

GRACIELA. You should save some of that money for yourself.

ALEX. It's for you guys.

GRACIELA. She'll suck you dry. She even wants a trip to the Canary Islands. She saw it on *Telemundo* and said, "It looks real pretty, *m'ija.*" *Papi* would be ashamed if he knew. I can still hear him. *(Quoting him)* "I am not a Mexican. I am not a wetback. You got to give me my minimum wage."

ALEX. What a jerk.

GRACIELA. I really believed that line about the welfare. Just an excuse to take off with that woman and her three kids.

ALEX. We're on vacation.

GRACIELA. Sometimes I think you live your whole life for him. Like all the hatred you have for him fuels you to want to be some big boxing champ. That is so twisted.

ALEX. I don't hate him. But I might be a little twisted.

GRACIELA. He'd be too embarrassed to come home.

ALEX. He's not coming home, Gracie.

GRACIELA. *(Wistfully)* It would be nice. If he did.

ALEX. Let him go.

GRACIELA. *(Beat)* Are you still fighting right before Cinco de Mayo even though you won in Hermosillo?

ALEX. Nope.

GRACIELA. Some guy from Brownsville got caught by the boxing commission playing both sides of the border and he lost his purse.

ALEX. Risk noted.

GRACIELA. Twenty-five K.

ALEX. Ouch.

GRACIELA. They repossessed the car he bought his mom. Had her grandson in the back seat and everything.

(Alex laughs.)

ALEX. You'll believe anything, won't you? Hey, enjoy the water and chill.

GRACIELA. I can't believe you won again. What's it like – to always win?

ALEX. I don't always win. Just most times.

(Alex giggles.)

GRACIELA. You're gonna be real famous someday.

ALEX. You think?

GRACIELA. Alex Moreno – the poster.

ALEX. Something for teenage girls to masturbate to.

GRACIELA. God, Alex.

ALEX. I fucked that guy up last night – kicked some *Mexicano* butt.

(Graciela touches his face. Last night left some marks. She starts their routine.)

GRACIELA. *(Affectionately)* You look like shit.

ALEX. So do you.

(Graciela laughs lightly. She starts embroidering one of three of Alex's boxing trunks.)

GRACIELA. *(Beat)* Aren't you worried that people are going to figure out you're not from Mexico? If you keep making mistakes with your Spanish; it's not *La boxeo* – you sound like a sissy.

ALEX. And they love the Magdalena thing because of Colosio. "If Colosio hadn't been shot down in Tijuana while he was running for president, then everything would have turned out beautiful." Like if he would've been president, he would've cleaned up the *pinche* government.

GRACIELA. He would have.

ALEX. Don't tell me you believe that shit.

GRACIELA. That's why he got assassinated, *pendejo*, because he would have cleaned up the *pinche* government.

ALEX. Okay, okay.

GRACIELA. So ignorant.

ALEX. Did you see those guys from Magdalena there acting like they knew me from school? They're like, "*¡Órale, vato!*" I love Mexico. It's okay to have a little pride. It's okay to lie to look good.

GRACIELA. I'm almost done.

(Alex reads the embroidery on the waistbands of his boxing trunks.)

ALEX. *(He likes this.)* Mi vida loca. ¿Te quiero?

GRACIELA. Well, you guys are always up there hugging and shit.

ALEX. *El bailador.* I'm not wearing that. It's a total *folklórico* thing.

GRACIELA. No one will know what it means.

ALEX. You just want to make me look like a wuss.

GRACIELA. You do dance. That's what they said in *KO Magazine.* "He's got the grace of a dancer and the swing of a – "

ALEX. "Tiger."

GRACIELA. Why'd they say that?

(Alex motions with his hand, indicating that ex-boxers have scrambled brains.)

ALEX. 'Cause they're written by ex-boxers.

(Graciela does not get it.)

They drag one leg, slur their words. Duh. Duh. Duh. You've seen *los veteranos* at the gym. You've seen Rainman.

GRACIELA. Rainman's not retarded?

ALEX. Hey, he had his day in the sun. He was regional champion. Three years in a row. But that was back when boxing was real dangerous. They used to schedule their fights too close together.

GRACIELA. *(Anxious)* Muhammed Ali *(got brain damage)* –

ALEX. I thought we'd retired Muhammed Ali.

GRACIELA. *Papi* had those tapes of Ali, remember?

ALEX. I thought we'd retired *Papi*, too.

GRACIELA. "Float like a butterfly and sting like a bee." Ali was our hero and look at him now.

ALEX. Ali has Parkinson's.

GRACIELA. What makes you so special that you think it's not going to happen to you?

ALEX. Hey, I am not Muhammed Ali here. Cassius Clay had a huge fat ego. He let himself take too many hits. Where as I wear boxing trunks that say *"Te quiero."* I am that *macho.* I am that confident. I am the only man *con huevos en mi familia.*

(Alex indicates his crotch.)

GRACIELA. You're pretty enamored with your balls.

ALEX. I'm not enamored.

GRACIELA. You grab them like they're gold or something.

(Alex laughs a special laugh that will echo later.)

ALEX. Hey, if I didn't have balls, I'd be a shitty boxer. And if I wasn't a boxer, we'd never get out of that hellhole. I'm gonna buy us a house far away from Barrio Hollywood. C'mon, a river with no water? Someone ought to condemn our entire street. I'm gonna give *Amá* everything she ever wanted and she'll forget about the past.

GRACIELA. Like everything with you has to be so profound.

(They stand and brush the sand off themselves, walking away from the water. They wave at their mother on the deck.)

ALEX. Hey, *Amá.*

(Graciela sees her and waves.)

AMÁ. *(O.S.)* That trip to the Canary Islands, Alex? Why don't we make it a cruise?

ALEX. *Lo que quieras, Mami.*

(Graciela nudges him.)

GRACIELA. Kiss up.

ALEX. You're cashing in on this, too.

GRACIELA. You know I don't care about money.

ALEX. What do you want for your 30th birthday?

GRACIELA. A dance studio with more room than the "Y," so I can teach my classes the steps I learned in Veracruz. Got enough money for that? And –

ALEX. What?

GRACIELA. You to dance *folklórico* with me again.

ALEX. Has it ever occurred to you to get someone else?

GRACIELA. Someone else isn't you. They don't understand.

ALEX. How do you know when you've never even looked for someone else. Take some risks, lil' sis. Get somebody new.

GRACIELA. They think it's wrong how much I love you, but I don't care. Just dance with me again, Alex. We dance so beautifully together. You know we do. C'mon.

ALEX. God, Gracie. Never. No fucking way.

GRACIELA. You don't have to hurt my feelings.

ALEX. Sometimes it seems like the only way to make you understand.

GRACIELA. Okay, I promise to never bring it up again.

ALEX. I bet.

(Graciela scoops up a handful of sand, sifts some of it into Alex's hand.)

GRACIELA. Here.

(He looks at it confused.)

A grain of sand for each promise.

(Alex puts the sand in his pocket.)

What are you doing?

ALEX. Keeping track.

(Graciela whacks him. They laugh. Lights fade on the beach.)

Scene 9

(The present. Inside the Moreno home. Lights come up on Amá who wears a large-brimmed straw hat and a Hawaiian short/top ensemble. She carries a suitcase. She sings to herself.)

AMÁ. *(Singing)* I love ME! Me. Me me.

(Graciela enters.)

GRACIELA. *(Singing)* You you you.

(Amá drops the suitcase.)

AMÁ. I was just…

GRACIELA. Having a love fest? *(Beat)* How's Alex doing?

AMÁ. He should be okay.

GRACIELA. Haven't you checked on him? I've got to get to rehearsal.

AMÁ. I poked my head in a few times. He was sleeping.

GRACIELA. *Amá*, he's been the same since he came home from the hospital. Unconscious. Where you headed?

AMÁ. *Nowheres.*

GRACIELA. Do you always pack to go nowhere?

AMÁ. Just dreaming.

GRACIELA. You pack to dream?

AMÁ. I'm dreaming again about the Canary Islands. Sitting in the shade with the canaries looking down at me. I packed my bags, my bathing suit, the first day of May. Alex had already given me some money, but I waited four days to see him fight. Four days and he would have $25,000. *(Short beat; suddenly upset)* I really want to go there.

GRACIELA. Maybe someday.

AMÁ. Maybe never. Because of Alex. *(Beat) Lo quiero tanto.*

GRACIELA. We both love him.

AMÁ. Even if his mind took a little break like that Dr. Morris said. But these things, this mind, can come back again. It can reappear. It's gray and fuzzy so it goes away, and then one day, it comes back and it's bright like a painting, *como el sol,* or that lipstick at the bottom of my purse. Red and alive. Like breathing. I keep waiting for that. For the red to come back to his face. But I can't wait anymore. I can't look at him in bed like that anymore.

GRACIELA. Do you think I want to look at him? We have to, *Amá.*

AMÁ. For how long?

GRACIELA. Forever.

AMÁ. Maybe if I go away, he'll wake up, like when you are really hungry at a restaurant and you go to the bathroom and you come back and your food is already there. Like a miracle. *(Beat)* Last night I turned him over. *(She points to her rear end.)* He had cuts right here. On his *nalgas.*

GRACIELA. I hope you put alcohol on those. They can get infected.

AMÁ. I –

GRACIELA. I'll do it.

AMÁ. I just can't –

GRACIELA. Shhh.

AMÁ. I'll go away, he'll get better. I know he will.

(Amá measures how small the vacation would be with her fingers.)

Un corto viaje. Para tu Mamá. (A little vacation for your mother.)

GRACIELA. It would be okay with me if we didn't have to take care of Alex.

AMÁ. I was looking forward to things like that. Taking classes. Making things with my hands.

GRACIELA. I know.

AMÁ. I wanted things, too. *Yo tenía sueños.* Just like you want your dance studio. *(Short beat)* I'll just be gone for a little bit. I can't help you anymore, *m'ija.* I can't help Alex. Let me go, so he can get better. I'll just close my eyes and God will make Alex well. Trust me, it will work.

GRACIELA. Don't leave us, too, *Amá.*

AMÁ. You have everything, *m'ija.* You have an Anglo doctor who loves you who won't run off with some *puta.*

GRACIELA. It's a little early to call it love.

AMÁ. You'd be crazy not to marry him. *(Beat)* I won't be long.

GRACIELA. *Amá,* you have to stay. Don't leave me here alone. Please.

(No response. Amá gives up.)

Promise you'll be here when I come back.

AMÁ. I promise.

(Graciela exits.)

Scene 10

(That night. The lighting gives the effect that there is something unreal about this place. Perhaps Michael is framed in blue light or in sharp edges. Michael wears pajamas and boxes fiercely. The only sounds we hear are Michael's grunts as he takes on a singular opponent. Alex, appears behind the scrim, boxing with a master's skill. Michael and Alex blend into one – a transference of power. Their physical movements, for a split second, mirror each other. It is as if Michael is possessed by the spirit of Alex.

The SOUND of ballet folklórico MUSIC comes up. When the music begins, Michael is thrown off balance. Graciela dances La Negra. Her moves have a direct impact on Michael and Alex's heads. The stomping of her feet becomes the pounding of their heads. The lines mimic what happens to them physically. It is no longer clear that Michael has a singular opponent, but multiple opponents, as he takes hits from all sides.)

MICHAEL. Trapped. Inside my body. Want out. Want freedom. From hand to head, nothing happens. Know how to take a punch – how to give one. Body stuck. Mind locked inside. Stuck. No freedom – can't speak – no voice. Better to drive on outta here. Drift on away.

(Alex disappears. Graciela enters in a white nightgown and lies down on the ground under a light cotton blanket. Michael has joined her under the blanket as though they were asleep for the night. A BOXING BELL RINGS. Michael jerks up, awakening from his dream. Graciela does not stir.

Michael instinctively gets up to check on Alex. Bleary-eyed and a little clumsy, Michael crosses into Alex's room. He is gone for several seconds.)

MICHAEL. Graciela!

(Graciela stirs, rolling over onto her side. Michael enters distraught.)

Graciela.

(*Graciela looks up at him.*)

Alex is dead.

(*Graciela leaps to her feet, pacing with her hands on her head. She stops moving, gathers her composure.*)

GRACIELA. *¡Amá! ¡Amá!*

(*Graciela goes to Amá's room. She comes out pale and a bit spooked after a long beat.*)

Oh, my God. She's gone.

(*Blackout.*)

End of Act I

ACT II

Scene 1

(The next day. Graciela leans in front of the outdoor barrio altar – El Tiradito. Graciela lights candles. It's a private moment. She is distraught – visibly shaken. In fact, her hand shakes so hard, she can hardly light the candle. The match goes out. Flustered, she lights another match. Michael enters.)

MICHAEL. Did you want me to get that for you?

(The match goes out when Graciela turns, startled to look at him.)

I didn't mean to startle you.

GRACIELA. I –

MICHAEL. Shh.

GRACIELA. I – I can't… see –

MICHAEL. Shh.

GRACIELA. – Him.

(Michael holds her.)

MICHAEL. It's time, Graciela. The police are ready for us.

GRACIELA. I keep…looking. I don't…see him.

MICHAEL. *(Comforting)* Shh.

GRACIELA. I saw him – every day. *(As if looking at Alex's face)* His face.

MICHAEL. I know.

GRACIELA. I never memorized him.

(She strikes her own heart.)

My heart –

(He holds her hand there.)

– forgot.

(Michael takes her hands.)

MICHAEL. Your mind remembers everything it's ever seen. It's the most amazing organ – the human brain.

GRACIELA. Not that amazing. When I get a scratch on my skin, my skin knows to grow back.

(Graciela leans on Michael as he leads her away.)

Scene 2

(Later that day. The police station. Graciela sits in a chair on stage right. Michael sits in a similar chair on stage left. It should be clear that these interviews are not happening in the same room although they are occurring simultaneously.)

GRACIELA. About 10 PM. That's when I last saw Alex alive.

MICHAEL. Her brother basically died the night of the fight. Sure, when she came into the hospital that day, I fell in love with her. I'm not going to defend that.

GRACIELA. Then, at about 10:30 my boyfriend, Michael, came to spend the night. *(Nervous laugh)* I don't usually have men over –

MICHAEL. Her love for her brother devastated her. I wanted to be part of a person who could love like that.

GRACIELA. You're not thinking Michael did this, are you? There's no chance that he did it. You don't understand what was going on.

MICHAEL. Maybe God just found a way to set Alex free.

GRACIELA. *(Beat)* But we didn't have the heart to do what he suggested.

MICHAEL. The doctor didn't bother to tell them what they could do.

GRACIELA. Maybe we should have. *(Beat)* Don't you know?

(Graciela looks up at them. They don't get it. She motions pulling an IV out of his arm.)

MICHAEL. To stop feeding him.

GRACIELA. Can you picture a family doing that?

MICHAEL. *(Agitated)* It happened because his mother had propped him up to watch Saturday Night Boxing on Mexican TV. His head fell back and got caught between the rails of the headboard.

GRACIELA. *(Reality starts dawning on her)* Oh, I have no idea where my mother went.

MICHAEL. *(Beat)* She's scared. She sure as hell isn't going to come here to talk to you.

GRACIELA. We acted like we never smelled him, but we did.

MICHAEL. A beautiful woman like Graciela all closed up in that house. It was a waste.

GRACIELA. Maybe my mom just stepped out for some fresh air – to talk to God. She'll be back.

MICHAEL. *(In love)* Graciela? How can anyone be objective about Graciela? You should see her dance. So much class. Like a queen. Made up perfectly like a photograph. Her hair pulled back tightly in a bun. And the eyes…

GRACIELA. *(Long beat)* She wanted to believe.

MICHAEL. The way I see it is Alex's mother made a simple mistake and Alex choked on the headboard. That's why his windpipe collapsed. Now, those two nice ladies get to go on with their lives. The whole thing just makes you want to have faith.

GRACIELA. See, where I come from, if you have faith, God has pity on you and makes things better. It's like He reaches His hand into your head and captures whatever picture you hold there. And if you imagine it just right, He'll set his hand down on earth and set that picture free. He makes it real. But you've got to believe. That's the first rule of faith. *(Beat)* My mother? She does what she wants. *(Realizing she's incriminated Amá)* Well, she wants what's best for us. Me and Alex. That's all I meant.

MICHAEL. Look, I'm a doctor. If I'm not willing to deal with the sick, I'm a hypocrite. *(Beat)* There is no murderer here.

GRACIELA. *(Upset)* Murder? My brother was a VEGETABLE. *(Beat)* Fucking *chota*.
Here. Why don't you arrest me instead? If you have to blame someone, why don't you blame me?

(Graciela offers her hands.)

Scene 3

(Later that day. Lights shift to Amá who enters hand-cuffed. It is clear she is in a separate space from the other two.)

AMÁ. My son. My child is dead. And you blame me? He killed him. Michael took Alex's throat in his hands and he killed him. I saw the whole thing. That horrible man murdered my son. I *am* a witness! I want that man to go to the electric chair! I want him dead! Let him feel what it feels like to be murdered. *(More upset)* My son was going to be fine. He had a difficult few months, but he was going to be fine. *(Short beat)* I did not sneak off. I went out for some air. *(Short beat)* No, I did not know he was dead when I left. I had no idea until you said it to me. What do you mean – contradicting myself? *(Beat)* You already have ideas in your head. I can see them floating around in there. I can see that! I didn't go to school. I don't have perfect English like you, but I can see this. This is not right. *(Short beat)* I saw everything. Don't pretend. When you know. *(Breaking down)* The truth.

Let me see Graciela. She knows why this happened. *(To herself)* Taking me from my church. From my prayers. When my God comforts me. That's who I love. That's who I listen to. *El siempre está conmigo.* You and your fancy cars. You and your guns. You've never done nothing good for me. *(Short beat; yelling to someone as if he's leaving)* Give me back my suitcase! My son gave me that. *Para mi cumpleaños.* For my birthday trip. He's giving it to me as a gift. When Graciela turns thirty, I turn forty-eight. Only two days apart. *(Getting emotional)* I saw that pretty island on Channel 52. I saw it in *Espanich.* It was a beautiful place with canaries up in the trees. And water – bluer than your eyes. You can see little canaries there like lizards in the desert. Singing all the time. Making everybody happy. And everybody could be happy if some people let God do His job.

(Amá starts crying.)

Simple things. That's all I ever wanted. *(Short beat)* I
didn't kill Alex with my hands but by wanting so much.
And he wanted so much to give me those things. He
fought when he was bleeding. When he couldn't see.
He fought for money. But I kept wanting more. And you
know how God feels about that! You must accept what
He gives you. And smile. BECAUSE THAT IS HOW
GOD WORKS! He makes the rules. He decides. And
you take it. Whatever hand you're dealt. But you gotta
keep your poker face on. You gotta look like you're
winning or you lose that much more. My grandfather
taught me that. He was a poker player from Chihua-
hua. He knew how to fool people into believing him.
(Quickly) That's not what I meant.

(Blackout.)

Scene 4

(A week later. Lights come up on the jail. Amá and Graciela are separated by a clear screen. Amá, dressed in an orange prison jumpsuit, looks around for bugs.)

GRACIELA. *Amá*, it's private. They assured me. No bugs.

AMÁ. You never know. I saw a *telenovela* once where this woman said something to her daughter in the *pinta* and they used it against her in court. They gave her the electric chair. Her hair was sticking up to the ceiling. Like this. *(She motions and laughs nervously.)*

GRACIELA. They're not gonna give you the electric chair. This case is totally bogus.

AMÁ. Who said so?

GRACIELA. I said so.

AMÁ. *(Registers disappointment)* They told me they want to put me in the prison. That I have to confess. I told them I'm guilty, but they want more. They want me to tell them every part. And I tell them, I don't remember. Every part. Only that I'm guilty, and I am, *m'ija*.

GRACIELA. We'll get you out of this.

AMÁ. How?

GRACIELA. We'll figure out a way.

AMÁ. I lied to them. I had to. Four hours they kept me in there. With no water. They didn't let me go to the bathroom. I had to pee! *(Beat)* They just kept telling me to sign that little piece of paper and everything would be all right. But I'm too smart for them. Too smart to fall for their tricks. I know the police here *thinks* you're supposed to call them first when somebody dies, but I couldn't do that. You can't trust *la chota*.

GRACIELA. You can't.

AMÁ. *(Slowly; whispering)* He was dead already when I left. But I don't think they need to know that. Why would they need to know?

(Amá looks around carefully to make sure no one is hearing her.)

That's why I went to the church. To talk to him. I missed him already. But we've missed him since Cinco de Mayo, ¿qué no? I just wanted to talk to him before all the craziness started. Before they took his body away. Because I saw this coming. I saw it ahead. Just like my *amá* used to see things and warn me before they happened. I could see the little pictures in my brain. And I didn't want them to be real for us. *Para nuestra familia.* But it's true. I put my hand on his neck and he was dead. His skin felt hard like a rock, and I lied about it.

GRACIELA. Why did you tell the police you saw Michael do it when you know he didn't?

AMÁ. I didn't stop him, *m'ija.* I didn't stop him because part of me wanted Alex to be dead. But it wasn't right. Alex should have died when God wanted him to die, not Michael.

GRACIELA. It wasn't Michael's fault.

AMÁ. He had ideas in his head. I hate him.

GRACIELA. I love him.

AMÁ. Promise me you'll never see him again. It's not right to turn your back on a sick person when you're supposed to be helping him.

GRACIELA. Maybe it was what had to be done – all that could be done. *(Tearing up)* Don't tell me you believe Alex was going to spring back to life and shower you with gifts? And kiss you on the cheek like you liked him to. He wasn't. He wasn't ever going to wake up again.

AMÁ. Michael left no place for God to do His miracle work. And God owed me one. He did. God was doing a miracle for Alex to make up for the years I spent with your father. *(Breaking down)* He owed me that. And He was this close to doing it. I could feel it. He was thinking about doing something special just for us, and Michael had to come in and spoil everything.

GRACIELA. Don't blame Michael. Alex's head fell back by itself. I don't see why we have to blame someone. Why does someone always have to take the responsibility?

AMÁ. I'm not afraid of taking the responsibility. I'm not afraid of dying.

GRACIELA. *(Beat; offhandedly)* Do you want me to just say that I did it so you can leave?

AMÁ. No. Don't lie to them. I already lied to them. We don't need you lying to them, too.

GRACIELA. *Amá,* I did –

AMÁ. It's a lie and I don't want to hear it again.

GRACIELA. – It would get you free.

AMÁ. *(Firmly)* No. I want to die. Maybe it would be a relief. I could just leave this earth. Like a breath.

GRACIELA. Don't say that.

AMÁ. I would see Alex again. At the end of a dark tunnel, there's a light. I read it in the *National Enquirer.* And all your *familia* waits for you there. Heaven – it's beautiful. The mountains and the trees. I could see him there. Again. I do love him. *(Back to reality)* Oh, I love you, too. You know that, don't you?

GRACIELA. I know.

AMÁ. Do you know how much?

GRACIELA. *(Crying)* I think I might.

AMÁ. It's hard to show you when I feel frozen inside. Like the meat in the freezer with little bits of ice in the cracks of my skin. I don't like this feeling, *m'ija*, because it is no feeling. *No siento nada.* I try and try to push my tears out, but there is no water left inside me.

GRACIELA. We cried a lot when he first got hurt. That's when we said goodbye.

AMÁ. *(Sighs)* I hate it here. They don't let me light my candles or nothing.

GRACIELA. I'll light one for you at home and at *El Tiradito,* too.

AMÁ. Would you?

GRACIELA. Of course. *(Crying)* I light a candle for you every night. I pray for you. Because I know you are innocent and someday you will come home.

(Amá looks up at the clock on the wall.)

AMÁ. Thank you for visiting your *amá*.

GRACIELA. *(Beat)* Let me change this.

AMÁ. You cannot change this.

GRACIELA. *(Beat)* You know I can.

AMÁ. *(Firmly)* You will not change this, Graciela.

GRACIELA. But –

AMÁ. *(Almost harsh)* Don't.

(It becomes clear Amá won't relent.)

GRACIELA. *(Conceding)* Okay, *wa*.

AMÁ. Don't let him into our lives again, *m'ija*. You and I do much better on our own. We do. We don't need some *gabacho* telling us what to do. We don't need some *gabacho* killing us in the middle of the night. I'd sleep better if you just let him go back where he belongs. Over there. *¿Verdad?* *(Beat)* Please. *(Firmly)* Do what I say.

(Graciela begins to walk away.)

Graciela.

Scene 5

(Later that day. El Tiradito. *Graciela is alone praying in front of the altar.)*

GRACIELA. You're not allowed to see me, so go away.

MICHAEL. That's not how you feel.

GRACIELA. *Amá* has her rules.

MICHAEL. You've broken them before. We made love in your bedroom. *(Short beat)* Three and a half times.

(Michael touches Graciela.)

(Emotionally) You love me.

GRACIELA. You need to go.

MICHAEL. *(Beat)* Does it bother you to feel something for me?

GRACIELA. I promised I wouldn't.

MICHAEL. You promised your mother you wouldn't love me? *(Beat)* Because she hallucinated I killed Alex?

(No response.)

You don't believe in that bullshit, do you?

GRACIELA. *(Softens)* I don't know what I know.

MICHAEL. *(Short beat)* You love me.

GRACIELA. I was starting to. I could feel it in there, like a little sprout trying to burst through the hard earth. A little flower in my heart, but you killed it.

MICHAEL. Well, mine was more than a sprout. It was kind of like a whole tree.

GRACIELA. Do you think true love can grow that fast?

MICHAEL. All I know is what I feel for you is pretty damn special. I want to feel that way forever.

GRACIELA. *(Fishing; calm)* Why'd you say Alex choked on the rails of the headboard?

MICHAEL. I didn't do it. You know I didn't.

GRACIELA. I just want to know why you said it.

MICHAEL. I was trying to protect your mother.

GRACIELA. *(Disappointed)* Oh.

MICHAEL. Why do you think I said it?

GRACIELA. They should let her come home. She deserves that, don't you think?

MICHAEL. She confessed, Graciela. Jesus. Of course they're going to hold her.

GRACIELA. She confessed because she feels guilty. *(Yells)* Because she has a conscience. Because of some fleeting thought she had one day.

MICHAEL. She feels guilty because she did it. It was her mistake.

GRACIELA. You don't understand us at all.

MICHAEL. I didn't want to see the police breathing down your throats because of some corpse with a heartbeat. That's why I made the headrail comment. I didn't off your brother. Frankly, I don't care why she did it. It was an asinine way to kill him. That is my only thought on the matter. *(Beat)* Someday, we could have a really beautiful life together. You and me.

(Graciela kisses him on the side of the mouth.)

GRACIELA. *(Solemn)* It's spoiled – paradise. It's like all the canaries have died and God doesn't live here anymore.

MICHAEL. You have no faith.

(Michael moves in closer to Graciela. She resists the attraction.)

GRACIELA. It wouldn't work anyway. You don't understand my language.

MICHAEL. I'm studying Spanish.

GRACIELA. That's not the language I'm talking about, Michael. The language of my heart. *(Beat)* My family moves in me. Like breathing itself.

MICHAEL. You're turning me down?

(Graciela remains tight, doesn't relent. Michael remains in disbelief.)

(Beat) I know how to love, Graciela. I'm a person who knows how to do that. You don't have a corner on love or family just because you're a Mexican. I have fought for your rights in this case. I have fought for the rights of your mother. I have fought. And if that isn't understanding the language of your heart, I don't know what is.

GRACIELA. Just leave.

MICHAEL. *(Long beat)* So, you're just going to rot away doing your dance classes forever? You're going to do that when you're sixty and you're living in poverty here in this fucked-up place?

GRACIELA. This fucked-up place is my home.

MICHAEL. I didn't mean – *(that)*.

GRACIELA. Sure, you meant. *(Beat)* I'm not going to be your pity-wife. *(Short beat)* So leave. I can clean up my own family's mess.

MICHAEL. *(Realizing)* Did you clean up your own family's mess?

GRACIELA. Leave.

MICHAEL. I love you anyway.

(Graciela watches him walk off. Blackout.)

Scene 6

(Lights up on Graciela at the police station. She has a bag full of visual aids. She pulls out specific items to punctuate her points. She is on stage alone facing the police detective.)

GRACIELA. Detective, you've gotta see this. I really think there's been some confusion here.

(She pulls the IV apparatus out of her bag and sets it on the table.)

He ate out of this.

(She sticks the bedpan on the table.)

He shit in this.

(She pulls out a sheet with red bloodstains.)

And if we didn't turn him enough, he'd bleed all over this. *(Beat)* You and your men combed my house for evidence. There just isn't any proof that my *Amá*, or anyone, calculated in any way to kill my brother. What do you have? A headrail. Evidence of some fanciful murder. Alex had his pride. He wouldn't have wanted his sister cleaning his bedpan. What do all these things prove, Detective?

To live you have to think. You have to laugh to be alive. *(Beat)* Alex was this miserable piece of flesh we prayed over. *(Beat)* How could God sit up there in heaven and watch us go through this and do absolutely nothing? *(Up to God)* How dare you, God? How dare you?

Oh, He's not there, I know, but I still like to pretend. *(Upset)* Because He used to bring me comfort.

(Blackout.)

Scene 7

(Later that day. Lights shift. Graciela is alone on stage in the semi-dark. She lights a candle with a picture of the Virgin of Guadalupe on it. She is in front of her altar.)

GRACIELA. *Amá's* free, *Virgen.* The cops let her go. Not enough evidence, I guess. I'm just letting you know what happened. In case you're not paying attention. In case you're too busy with India or the Middle East or something. In case other people in the world have problems that are so much worse than ours.

Is it true, *Virgencita?* Do you always forgive like *Amá* says? Will the words I speak on earth be swept up with the wind and somehow catch your ear in heaven? *(Beat)* You wouldn't punish me for wanting us to be free, would you? For wanting to dance – to hear their applause. Every time they put their hands together, I feel it in my heart like one very loud beat.

(Graciela claps her hands together, once and slowly.)

And I keep on living.

(Beat) I can't sleep. Not since that night. *(Beat)* Do you really spy on us from behind your cloud like *Amá* says? *(Long beat)* You could let me know if you do. You could bring me roses in winter or something. Like you did for Juan Diego. To help me believe.

(Graciela lifts the candle skyward.)

Can you see my little candle? It's just one tiny light and the world is so big. Free me. Like you did her. Free me. From that picture of what I did to him stuck in my mind. *Virgen,* I want you to know that I loved my brother. With everything inside me. And if there is anyway in your great big heart that you can find a space for me, where I can sit and rest for a moment, I ask that you let me in there.

(Graciela closes her eyes in prayer. Alex enters. They are now inside the Virgin's heart – red, pink and beating. Graciela opens her eyes and sees him.)

(Hard to say) I...killed you.

ALEX. I thought I recognized that half-ass manicure job.

GRACIELA. It's not funny.

ALEX. You were praying for forgiveness.

GRACIELA. They would have left you unconscious forever. We would never have danced again. Could you see me with my feet pinned to the ground? You – pinned to a body that couldn't move?

ALEX. Heaven's better. Tougher boxers.

GRACIELA. *(A tizzy)* I'm imagining you, right? Because I haven't slept. I'm trying to get strong. Trying not to die. Dying seems so easy sometimes – dying seems like it sneaks right up on you when you're not paying attention.

Do you forgive me?

(Alex nods. She touches Alex.)

You're back. *(Beat)* I can see you in my mind again. And you're not the way you were at the hospital at all. *(Delighting in the memory)* But you're bright and awake. And we're laughing like we used to. We're getting ready to perform and we're standing in the dressing room and my hair is all stiff from the hairspray. And my face is red from the rouge. And you're putting on your pants, trying not to notice that every girl there, except me, is watching you buckle yourself. You tap your foot. That's my cue. It's just a simple tap at first.

(Alex starts to tap his foot. It is the beginning of a simple ballet folklórico step. Graciela begins to slowly tap in unison with him. She stops.)

I have to call the police. I have to turn myself in.

ALEX. I can see things now I never imagined. I can see your soul.

GRACIELA. Does it have like a big black stain on it?

ALEX. No.

(Graciela opens her mouth to protest.)

You'll just have to trust me on that.

GRACIELA. *(Beat)* Did you ever feel like you failed the one person you loved most in the world?

ALEX. I was never going to wake up again. It was brave what you did, but you always were my protector – the one. The only one I could count on. In this life. *For reals.*

GRACIELA. I feel like you're leaving me.

ALEX. I am.

GRACIELA. In Barrio Hollywood, you will always be alive to me. Like a lively ghost. With hands and feet. Who sometimes likes to dance. Who strokes your face when you're crying. Who grasps your hand when you feel alone. *(Beat)* Don't go yet.

ALEX. Gracie, we're dance partners. I'm a part of you and you're a part of me.

(Alex strokes Graciela's face as she is crying and grasps her hand. He kisses her goodbye.)

GRACIELA. Did I ever tell you I love you, little bro?

ALEX. *(He giggles; beat)* You know what would really make me happy, Gracie? If you let yourself love somebody else.

GRACIELA. But I love you.

ALEX. Somebody who isn't family.

GRACIELA. They don't understand – when they're not family.

ALEX. Somebody alive.

(Alex hands her some sand.)

GRACIELA. *(Surprised)* Sand? A grain of sand for each promise.

ALEX. You can do it. I know you can.

(As he walks off –)

GRACIELA. Just one more dance, Alex. Just one more dance.

(– but it is too late for him to answer and the Virgin's heart disappears.)

Scene 8

(Moreno home. Michael bumps into Amá while she is outside watering the plants. Amá crosses back into the house without saying a word. Graciela hangs up a paper cut-out streamer that says "Welcome Home.")

GRACIELA. Go back out there. I'm not done yet.

AMÁ. He's out there.

GRACIELA. I didn't invite him over.

MICHAEL. *(Still outside)* I love her!

(Graciela hears this from inside the house. She can't help but smile. Amá seems less jubilant than she was during her release.)

AMÁ. Screaming out there. For all the neighbors to hear.

(Graciela starts to leave.)

Don't – *(go)*

(Graciela opens the door.)

GRACIELA. I'm just gonna… tell him to leave.

(Graciela steps outside.)

Hi.

MICHAEL. Hi.

GRACIELA. You came back.

MICHAEL. Didn't know where else to go really. Just wandering around out there. In the desert. Driving.

GRACIELA. Do you wanna come in? Actually, let's just stay out here.

MICHAEL. Okay.

(Michael and Graciela sit on the top step of the wooden porch. The night sky has made a display of stars. He takes her hand.)

Feels good – holding your hand.

GRACIELA. Yeah.

MICHAEL. I'm sorry.

GRACIELA. No, I'm sorry.

MICHAEL. Most women would give up after a fight like that.

GRACIELA. *(Long beat)* Do you think killing your little brother is love?

MICHAEL. It can be. The truest, purest act of love.

GRACIELA. "Thou shall not kill." One of the Ten Commandments.

MICHAEL. When they hang on like that, it can go on for years. And it's the family who suffers. You did the right thing.

GRACIELA. It was an asinine way to do it.

MICHAEL. You're a woman who knows how to love, Graciela. You're a person who knows how to do that.

GRACIELA. *(Touched)* Stop. *(Beat)* It's hard. To let yourself love somebody... different. *(Beat)* It's hard. *(Beat)* For me. *(Beat)* But I love you. Phew! I've never said that to a man before.

MICHAEL. I don't believe that.

GRACIELA. *(An admission)* It feels like I've never said it before.

MICHAEL. I love you, too.

GRACIELA. *(Beat)* You're really different from us, but you know you are. That's what makes you special.

MICHAEL. *(Beat)* Is your *Amá* gonna have trouble if we get back together?

GRACIELA. Yeah.

MICHAEL. *(Disappointed)* Oh.

GRACIELA. Just because it's hard doesn't mean we shouldn't do it.

MICHAEL. Does she know what really happened?

GRACIELA. Little girls don't commit murder. I'm supposed to agree that you did it.

MICHAEL. Wow.

GRACIELA. It's complicated family stuff.

MICHAEL. I understand.

GRACIELA. I don't think it will ever come up again if that helps.

MICHAEL. Okay, *wa.*

(Graciela laughs.)

GRACIELA. Now, we got you saying *"wa."*

MICHAEL. I've always said *wa.*

(There's an awkward silence. Then, they relax more into the silence. They look at the sky.)

GRACIELA. *(Beat)* If you could do one thing in the whole world that you've never done before, what would it be?

MICHAEL. Let me think.

GRACIELA. C'mon, you're not supposed to think. You're supposed to just say it.

MICHAEL. I can't just say it. That's not the way my mind works.

GRACIELA. Come on. Blurt.

MICHAEL. *(Long beat)* I'd learn to dance the dance with you. I'd hold my head in place and have that serious look, and have my hand against my waist right over my belt buckle, and you would find me attractive. And nobody would say, "What's that white guy doing up there dancing like that?" Nobody would even notice. They would just see two people dancing and they would know I'm a part of you and you're a part of me.

(The echo of Alex's words moves Graciela. Graciela kisses him gently. A quiet moment.)

GRACIELA. *(Long beat)* Listen. Can you hear… my little brother laugh?

(Michael strains to hear, gives up.)

MICHAEL. I guess I don't live in the magical world that you do.

(Graciela grabs Michael's hand.)

GRACIELA. Stay with me. And you will.

(In the distance, there is the faint sound of Alex's laugh. Michael registers it. Graciela stands and pulls Michael toward her, teaching him the first steps of the ballet folklórico *dance she danced earlier with Alex. In the Tucson night sky, a storm brews. The thunderous CRACK of a summer thunderstorm. Lightning lights up the sky. A light rain begins FALLING.*

As they dance in the rain, lights dim. Alex's laugh CRACKS again and grows faint, but they don't hear it as they are wrapped up in each other. Lights fade to black.)

End of Play

SET

Mexican flag (Act 1, Scene 1)

Ropes of a boxing ring, or elements to imply a boxing ring (Act 1, Scene 1)

Partial lime green wall, or elements to imply the hospital (Act 1, Scene 2)

Altar table (Act 1, Scene 2)

Scrim (Act 1, Scene 2)

Kitchen table (Act 1, Scene 4)

Window frame (Act 1, Scene 4)

Steps of a porch (Act 1, Scene 5 and Act 2, Scene 8)

Couch (Act 1, Scene 6)

Upside down boat (partial) (Act 1, Scene 8)

Second story deck (partial) (Act 1, Scene 8)

Outside barrio altar with a partial adobe wall (El Tiradito, Tucson, Arzona) (Act 2, Scene 1 and Act 2, Scene 5)

Two chairs (Act 2, Scene 2)

A partial wall separating the two chairs (Act 2, Scene 2)

A clear screen to separate the prisoner from the visitor at the jail (Act 2, Scene 4)

Clock on the wall (Act 2, Scene 4)

COSTUMES

Boxing trunks (ALEX, Act 1, Scene 1)

Boxing gloves (ALEX, Act 1, Scene 1)

White ballet folklórico dress (Veracruz style) (GRACIELA, Act 1,
    Scene 1 and Act 1, Scene 6)

Ballet folklórico headresss with a candle on it, used for the dance, La
    Bruja (from Veracruz), (GRACIELA, Act 1, Scene 1)

Fake braid, (GRACIELA, Act 1, Scene 1 and Act 1, Scene 6)

Physician's white lab coat (MICHAEL Act 1, Scene 2)

White shirt with collar (MICHAEL Act 1, Scene 2)

Ballet folklórico headdress with a broken candle on it (GRACIELA,
    Act 1, Scene 6)

Woman's bathing suit with sarong (GRACIELA, Act 1, Scene 8)

Men's bathing suit with pockets (Alex, Act 1, Scene 8)

Women's straw hat (AMA, Act 1, Scene 9)

Hawaiian shorts and top (AMA, Act 1, Scene 9)

Men's pajamas (MICHAEL, Act 1, Scene 10)

Yellow ballet folklórico dress with red trim (Jalisco style) for La Negra
    (GRACIELA Act 1, Scene 10)

Woman's orange jail jumpsuit (AMA, Act 2, Scene 3)

PROP LIST

Small votive candle in blue glass (AMA, Act 1, Scene 2)
Handkerchief (AMA, Act 1, Scene 2)
Cigarette lighter (AMA, Act 1, Scene 2)
Salt shaker (AMA, Act 1, Scene 2)
Rosary (AMA, Act 1, Scene 2)
Medical chart (MICHAEL, Act 1, Scene 2)
Stethoscope (MICHAEL, Act 1, Scene 2)
Lipstick (AMA, Act 1, Scene 2)
Long wooden match (AMA, Act 1, Scene 3)
Box of long wooden matches (AMA, Act 1, Scene 3)
Virgin of Guadalupe Candle (AMA, Act 1, Scene 3)
Blue star-studded cloth (AMA, Act 1, Scene 3)
Hospital bed with wheels (ALEX, Act 1, Scene 4)
Intravenous feeding tube (ALEX, Act 1, Scene 4)
White sheets (ALEX, Act 1, Scene 4)
White pillows (ALEX, Act 1, Scene 4)
Casserole dish (AMA, Act 1, Scene 4)
Small salad bowl (AMA, Act 1, Scene 4)
Several religious candles (GRACIELA, Act 1, Scene 4)
Fork (AMA, Act 1, Scene 4)
Plates (MICHAEL, Act 1, Scene 4)
Boom Box (GRACIELA, Act 1, Scene 5)
Backpack (GRACIELA, Act 1, Scene 5)
Man's ballet folklórico belt (GRACIELA, Act 1, Scene 5, Act 2, Scene 8)
Book with the title, Boxing and Medicine: Head Trauma and the
    Pugilitic Patient (GRACIELA, Act 1, Scene 5)
Vacuum cleaner wrapped in a red bow (AMA, Act 1, Scene 6)
Necklace with a crucifix (GRACIELA, Act 1, Scene 6)
Razor (AMA, Act 1, Scene 6)
Purse (AMA, Act 1, Scene 6)
Pair of boxing trunks (AMA, Act 1, Scene 6)
Scale (AMA, Act 1, Scene 6)
Small pink candle encased in glass (AMA, Act 1, Scene 6)
Medical tape (ALEX, Act 1, Scene 6)
Embroidered boxing trunks (GRACIELA, Act 1, Scene 8)
Suitcase (AMA, Act 1, Scene 9)
Light cotton blanket (MICHAEL, Act 1, Scene 10)
A religious candle (GRACIELA, Act 2, Scene 1)
A book of matches (GRACIELA, Act 2, Scene 1)
Handcuffs (AMA, Act 2, Scene 3)
A bag full of visual aids (GRACIELA, Act 2, Scene 6)
IV apparatus (GRACIELA, Act 2, Scene 6)
Bedpan (GRACIELA, Act 2, Scene 6)
Blood-stained sheet (GRACIELA, Act 2, Scene 6)
Virgin of Guadalupe candle (GRACIELA, Act 2, Scene 7)
Watering can (AMA, Act 2, Scene 8)
Cut-out paper streamer that reads, "Welcome Home" (GRACIELA,
    Act 2, Scene 8)